La Fiammetta

Giovanni Boccaccio

Table of Contents

La Fiammetta

Giovanni Boccaccio

Kessinger Publishing reprints thousands of hard–to–find books!

Visit us at http://www.kessinger.net

LA FIAMMETTA

BY

GIOVANNI BOCCACCIO

TRANSLATED BY JAMES C. BROGAN

1907.

INTRODUCTION

Youth, beauty, and love, wit, gayety and laughter, are the component parts of the delightful picture conjured up by the mere name of Giovanni Boccaccio, the prince of story–tellers for all generations of men. This creator of a real literary epoch was born in Paris, in 1313, (in the eleventh year of Dante's exile), of an Italian father and a French–woman of good family. His father was a merchant of Florence, whither he returned with his son when the child was seven years old. The boy received some education, but was placed in a counting–house when he was only thirteen, and at seventeen he was sent by his father to Naples to enter another commercial establishment. But he disliked commerce, and finally persuaded his father to allow him to study law for two years at the University of Naples, during which period the lively and attractive youth made brisk use of his leisure time in that gay and romantic city, where he made his way into the highest circles of society, and unconsciously gleaned the material for the rich harvest of song and story that came with his later years. At this time he was present at the coronation of the poet Petrarch in the Capitol, and was fired with admiration for the second greatest poet of that day. He chose Petrarch for his model and guide, and in riper manhood became his most intimate friend.

By the time he was twenty–five, Boccaccio had fallen in love with the Lady Maria, a natural daughter of King Robert of Naples, who had caused her to be adopted as a member of the family of the Count d'Aquino, and to be married when very young to a Neapolitan nobleman. Boccaccio first saw her in the Church of San Lorenzo on the morning of Easter eve, in 1338, and their ensuing friendship was no secret to their world. For the entertainment of this youthful beauty he wrote his *Filicopo*, and the fair Maria is undoubtedly the heroine of several of his stories and poems. His father insisted upon his return to Florence in 1340, and after he had settled in that city he occupied himself seriously with literary work, producing, between the years 1343 and 1355, the *Teseide* (familiar to English readers as "The Knight's Tale" in Chaucer, modernized by Dryden as "Palamon and Arcite"), *Ameto, Amorosa Visione, La Fiammetta, Ninfale Fiesolona*, and his most famous work, the *Decameron*, a collection of stories written, it is said, to amuse Queen Joanna of Naples and her court, during the period when one of the world's greatest plagues swept over Europe in 1348. In these years he rose from the vivid but confused and exaggerated manner of *Filocopo* to the perfection of polished literary style. The *Decameron* fully revealed his genius, his ability to weave the tales of all lands and all ages into one harmonious whole; from the confused mass of legends of the Middle Ages, he evolved a world of human interest and dazzling beauty, fixed the kaleidoscopic picture of Italian society, and set it in the richest frame of romance.

While he had the *Decameron* still in hand, he paused in that great work, with heart full of passionate longing for the lady of his love, far away in Naples, to pour out his very soul in *La Fiammetta*, the name by which he always called the Lady Maria. Of the real character of this lady, so famous in literature, and her true relations with Boccaccio, little that is certain is known. In several of his poems and in the *Decameron* he alludes to her as being cold as a marble statue, which no fire can ever warm; and there is no proof, notwithstanding the ardor of Fiammetta as portrayed by her lover—who no doubt wished her to become the reality of his glowing picture—that he ever really received from the charmer whose name was always on his lips anything more than the friendship that was apparent to all the world. But she certainly inspired him in the writing of his best works.

The best critics agree in pronouncing *La Fiammetta* a marvelous performance. John Addington Symonds says: "It is the first attempt in any literature to portray subjective emotion exterior to the writer; since the days of Virgil and Ovid, nothing had been essayed in this region of mental analysis. The author of this extraordinary work proved himself a profound anatomist of feeling by the subtlety with which he dissected a woman's heart." The story is full of exquisite passages, and it exercised a widespread and lasting influence over all the narrative literature that followed it. It is so rich in material that it furnished the motives of many tales, and the novelists of the sixteenth century availed themselves freely of its suggestions.

After Boccaccio had taken up a permanent residence in Florence, he showed a lively interest in her political affairs, and fulfilled all the duties of a good citizen. In 1350 he was chosen to visit the lords of various towns of Romagna, in order to engage their cooperation in a league against the Visconti family, who, already lords of the great and powerful city of Milan, desired to extend their domains beyond the Apennines. In 1351 Boccaccio had the pleasure of bearing to the poet Petrarch the news of the restoration of his rights of citizenship and of his patrimony, both of which he had lost in the troubles of 1323, and during this visit the two geniuses became friends for life. They delved together into the literature of the ancients, and Boccaccio determined, through the medium of translation, to make the work of the great Greek writers a part of the liberal education of his countrymen. A knowledge of Greek at that time was an exceedingly rare accomplishment, since the serious study of living literatures was only just beginning, and the Greek of Homer had been almost forgotten. Even Petrarch, whose erudition was marvelous, could not read a copy of the *Iliad* that he possessed. Boccaccio asked permission of the Florentine Government to establish a Greek professorship in the University of Florence, and persuaded a learned Calabrian, Leonzio Pilato, who had a perfect knowledge of ancient Greek, to leave Venice and accept the professorship at Florence, and lodged him in his own house. Together the Calabrian and the author of *La Fiammetta* and the *Decameron* made a Latin translation of the *Iliad*, which Boccaccio transcribed with his own hand. But his literary enthusiasm was not confined to his own work and that of the ancients. His soul was filled with a generous ardor of admiration for Dante; through his efforts the Florentines were awakened to a true sense of the merits of the sublime poet, so long exiled from his native city, and the younger genius succeeded in persuading them to establish a professorship in the University for the sole study of the *Divine Comedy*, he himself being the first to occupy the chair, and writing a *Life of Dante*, besides commentaries on the *Comedy* itself.

Mainly through his intimacy with the spiritual mind of Petrarch, Boccaccio's moral character gradually underwent a change from the reckless freedom and unbridled love of pleasure into which he had easily fallen among his associates in the court life at Naples. He admired the delicacy and high standard of honor of his friend, and became awakened to a sense of man's duty to the world and to himself. During the decade following the year 1365 he occupied himself at his home in Certaldo, near Florence, with various literary labors, often entertaining there the great men of the world.

Petrarch's death occurred in 1374, and Boccaccio survived him but one year, dying on the twenty–first of December, 1375. He was buried in Certaldo, in the Church of San Michele e Giacomo.

That one city should have produced three such men as the great triumvirate of the fourteenth century—Dante, Petrarch, Boccaccio—and that one half–century should have witnessed their successive triumphs, is the greatest glory of Florence, and is one of the most notable facts in the history of genius.

We quote once more from Symonds: "Dante brought the universe into his *Divine Comedy*. 'But the soul of man, too, is a universe', and of this inner microcosm Petrarch was the poet and genius. It remained for Boccaccio to treat of daily life with an art as

5

La Fiammetta

distinct and dazzling as theirs. From Dante's Beatrice, through Petrarch's Laura, to Boccaccio's La Fiammetta—from woman as an allegory of the noblest thoughts and purest stirrings of the soul, through woman as the symbol of all beauty worshiped at a distance, to woman as man's lover, kindling and reciprocating the most ardent passion; from mystic, stately periods to Protean prose; from verse built up into cathedral–like dignity, through lyrics light as arabesques and pointed with the steely touch of polished style, to that free form of speech which takes all moods and lends itself alike to low or lofty things—such was the rapid movement of Italian genius within the brief space of fifty years. So quickly did the Renaissance emerge from the Middle Ages; and when the voices of that august trio were silenced in the grave, their echoes ever widened and grew louder through the spacious time to come."

No translation into English of *La Fiammetta* has been made since Shakespeare's time—when a small edition was published, which is now so rare as to be practically unattainable—until the appearance of the present Scholarly and poetic rendering, which places within the reach of all one of the world's greatest masterpieces of literature.

D.K.R.

La Fiammetta

PROLOGUE

Beginneth the Book called Elegy of Madonna Fiammetta, sent by her to Ladies in Love.

When the wretched perceive or feel that their woes arouse compassion, their longing to give vent to their anguish is thereby increased. And so, since, from long usance, the cause of my anguish, instead of growing less, has become greater, the wish has come to me, noble ladies—in whose hearts, mayhap, abides a love more fortunate than mine—to win your pity, if I may, by telling the tale of my sorrows. Nor is it at all my intent that these my words should come to the ears of men. Nay, rather would I, so far as lies in my power, withhold my complaints from them; for, such bitterness has the discovery of the unkindness of one man stirred in me, that, imagining all other men to be like him, methinks I should be a witness of their mocking laughter rather than of their pitying tears. You alone do I entreat to peruse my story, knowing full well that you will feel with me, and that you have a pious concern for others' pangs. Here you will not find Grecian fables adorned with many lies, nor Trojan battles, foul with blood and gore, but amorous sentiments fed with torturing desires. Here will appear before your very eyes the dolorous tears, the impetuous sighs, the heart–breaking words, the stormy thoughts, which have harrowed me with an ever–recurring goad, and have torn away from me sleep and appetite and the pleasant times of old, and my much–loved beauty. When you behold these things, and behold them with the ardent feelings which ladies are wont to have, sure I am that the cheeks of each separately, and of all when brought together, will be bathed in tears, because of those ills which are alone the occasion of my never–ending misery. Do not, I beseech you, refuse me these tears, reflecting that your estate is unstable as well as mine, and that, should it ever come to resemble mine (the which may God forfend!), the tears that others shed for you will be pleasing to you in return. And that the time may pass more rapidly in speaking than in, weeping, I will do my best to fulfil my promise briefly, beginning with that love which was more happy than lasting, so that, by comparing that happiness with my present case, you may learn that I am now more unhappy than any woman ever has been. And afterward I will trace with mournful pen, as best I can, all the agonies which are justly the source of my lamentations. But first, if the prayers of the wretched are heard, if there is in Heaven any Deity whose holy mind can be touched with compassion for me, afflicted as I am, bathed in my own tears, Him I beseech to aid my despondent memory and support my trembling hand in its present task. So may the tortures which I have felt and still feel in my soul become fruitful, and the memory will suggest the words for them, and the hand, more eager than apt for such duty, will write them down.

Chapter I

Wherein the lady describes who she was, and by what signs her misfortunes were foreshadowed, and at what time, and where, and in what manner, and of whom she became enamored, with the description of the ensuing delight.

In the time when the newly-vestured earth appears more lovely than during all the rest of the year came I into the world, begotten of noble parents and born amid the unstinted gifts of benignant fortune. Accursed be the day, to me more hateful than any other, on which I was born! Oh, how far more befitting would it have been had I never been born, or had I been carried from that luckless womb to my grave, or had I possessed a life not longer than that of the teeth sown by Cadmus, or had Atropos cut the thread of my existence at the very hour when it had begun! Then, in earliest childhood would have been entombed the limitless woes that are the melancholy occasion of that which I am writing. But what boots it to complain of this now? I am here, beyond doubt; and it has pleased and even now pleases God that I should be here. Born and reared, then, amid boundless affluence, I learned under a venerable mistress whatever manners and refinements it beseems a demoiselle of high rank to know. And as my person grew and developed with my increasing years, so also grew and developed my beauty. Alas! even while a child, on hearing that beauty acclaimed of many, I gloried therein, and cultivated it by ingenious care and art. And when I had bidden farewell to childhood, and had attained a riper age, I soon discovered that this, my beauty —ill-fated gift for one who desires to live virtuously!—had power to kindle amorous sparks in youths of my own age, and other noble persons as well, being instructed thereupon by nature, and feeling that love can be quickened in young men by beauteous ladies. And by divers looks and actions, the sense of which I did but dimly discern at the time, did these youths endeavor in numberless ways to kindle in my heart the fire wherewith their own hearts glowed—fire that was destined, not to warm, but rather to consume me also in the future more than it ever has burned another woman; and by many of these young men was I sought in marriage with most fervid and passionate entreaty. But after I had chosen among them one who was in every respect congenial to me, this importunate crowd of suitors, being now almost hopeless, ceased to trouble me with their looks and attentions. I, therefore, being satisfied, as was meet, with such a husband, lived most happily, so long as fervid love, lighted by flames hitherto unfelt, found no entrance into my young soul. Alas! I had no wish unsatisfied; nothing that could please me or any other lady ever was denied me, even for a moment. I was the sole delight, the peculiar felicity of a youthful spouse, and, just as he loved me, so did I equally love him. Oh, how much happier should I have been than all other women, if the love for him that was then in my heart had endured!

It was, then, while I was living in sweet content, amid every kind of enjoyment, that Fortune, who quickly changes all things earthly, becoming envious of the very gifts which she herself had bestowed, withdrew her protecting hand. At first uncertain in what manner she could succeed in poisoning my happiness, she at length managed, with subtle craft, to make mine own very eyes traitors and so guide me into the path that led to disaster. But the gods were still propitious to me, nay, were even more concerned for my fate than I myself. Having seen through her veiled malice, they wished to supply me with weapons, had I but known how to avail me thereof, wherewith I might fend my breast, and not go unarmed to the battle wherein I was destined to fall. Yea, on the very night that preceded the day which was the beginning of all my woes, they revealed to me the future in my sleep by means of a clear and distinct vision, in such wise as follows:

While lying on my spacious couch, with all my limbs relaxed in deepest slumber, I seemed to be filled with greater joy than I had ever felt before, and wherefore I knew not. And the day whereon this happened was the brightest and loveliest of days. I was standing alone in verdant grass, when, with the joy whereof I spoke, came the thought to me that it might be well for me to repose in a meadow that appeared to be shielded from the fervid rays of the sun by the shadows cast by various trees newly garbed in their glossy foliage. But first, gathering divers flowers, wherewith the whole sward was bejeweled, I placed them, with my white hands, in a corner of my robe, and then, sitting down and choosing flower after flower, I wove therefrom a fair garland, and adorned my head with it. And, being so adorned, I arose, and, like unto Proserpine at what time Pluto ravished her from her mother, I went along singing in this new springtime. Then, being perchance weary, I laid me down in a spot where the verdure was deepest and softest. But, just as the tender foot of Eurydice was pierced by the concealed viper, so meseemed that a hidden serpent came upon me, as I lay stretched on the grass, and pierced me under the left breast. The bite of the sharp fang, when it first entered, seemed to burn me. But afterward, feeling somewhat reassured, and yet afraid of something worse ensuing, I thought I clasped the cold serpent to my bosom, fancying that by communicating to it the warmth of that bosom, I should thereby render it more kindly disposed in my regard in return for such a service. But the viper, made bolder and more obdurate by that very favor, laid his hideous mouth on the wound he had given me, and after a long space, and after it had drunk much of my blood, methought that, despite my resistance, it drew forth my soul; and then, leaving my breast, departed with it. And at the very moment of the serpent's departure the day lost its brightness, and a thick shadow came behind me and covered me all over, and the farther the serpent crept, the more lowering grew the heavens, and it seemed almost as if the reptile dragged after it in its course the masses of thick, black clouds that appeared to follow in its wake, Not long afterward, just as a white stone flung into deep water gradually vanishes from the eyes of the beholder, so it, too, vanished from my sight. Then the heavens became darker and darker, and I thought that the sun had suddenly withdrawn and night had surely returned, as it had erstwhile returned to the *Greeks* because of the crime of Atrcus. Next, flashes of lightning sped swiftly along the skies, and peals of crashing thunder appalled the earth and me likewise. And through all, the wound made in my breast by the bite of the serpent remained with me still, and full of viperous poison; for no medicinal help was within my reach, so that my entire body appeared to have swollen in a most foul and disgusting manner. Whereupon I, who before this seemed to be without life or motion—why, I do not know—feeling that the force of the venom was seeking to reach my heart in divers subtle ways, now tossed and rolled upon the cool grass, expecting death at any moment. But methought that when the hour of my doom arrived, I was struck with terror at its approach, and the anguish of my heart was so appalling, while looking forward to its coming, that my inert body was convulsed with horror, and so my deep slumber was suddenly broken. No sooner was I fully awake than, being still alarmed by the things I had seen, I felt with my right hand for the wound in my breast, searching at the present moment for that which was already being prepared for my future misery. Finding that no wound was there, I began to feel quite safe and even merry, and I made a mock of the folly of dreams and of those who believe in them, and so I rendered the work of the gods useless. Ah, wretched me! if I mocked them then, I had good reason to believe in them afterward, to my bitter sorrow and with the shedding of useless tears; good reason had I also to complain of the gods, who reveal their secrets to mortals in such mystic guise that the things that are to happen in the future can hardly be said to be revealed at all. Being then fully awake, I raised my drowsy head, and, as soon as I saw the light of the new-risen sun enter my chamber, laying aside every other thought directly, I at once left my couch.

That day, too, was a day of the utmost solemnity for almost everyone. Therefore, attiring myself carefully in glittering cloth of gold, and adorning every part of my person with deft and cunning hand, I made ready to go to the August festival, appareled like unto the goddesses seen by Paris in the vale of Ida. And, while I was lost in admiration of myself, just as the peacock is of his plumage, imagining that the delight which I took in my own appearance would surely be shared by all who saw me, a flower from my wreath fell on the ground near the curtain of my bed, I know not wherefore—perhaps plucked from my head by a celestial hand by me unseen. But I, careless of the occult signs by which the gods forewarn mortals, picked it up, replaced it on my head, and, as if nothing portentous had happened, I passed out from my abode. Alas! what clearer token of what was to befall me could the gods have given me? This should have served to prefigure to me that my soul, once free and sovereign of itself, was on that day to lay aside its sovereignty and become a slave, as it betided. Oh, if my mind had not been distempered, I should have surely known that to me that day would be the blackest and direst of days, and I should have let it pass without ever crossing the threshold of my home! But although the gods usually hold forth signs whereby those against whom they are incensed may be warned, they often deprive them of due understanding; and thus, while pointing out the path they ought to follow, they at the same time sate their own anger. My ill fortune, then, thrust me forth from my house, vain and careless that I was; and, accompanied by several ladies, I moved with slow step to the sacred temple, in which the solemn function required by the day was already celebrating. Ancient custom, as well as my noble estate, had reserved for me a prominent place among the other ladies. When I was seated, my eyes, as was my habit of old, quickly wandered around the temple, and I saw that it was crowded with men and women, who were divided into separate groups. And no sooner was it observed that I was in the temple than (even while the sacred office was going on) that happened which had always happened at other times, and not only did the men turn their eyes to gaze upon me, but the women did the same, as if Venus or Minerva had newly descended from the skies, and would never again be seen by them in that spot where I was seated. Oh, how often I laughed within my own breast, being enraptured with myself, and taking glory unto myself because of such things, just as if I were a real goddess! And so, nearly all the young gentlemen left off admiring the other ladies, and took their station around me, and straightway encompassed me almost in the form of a complete circle; and, while speaking in divers ways of my beauty, each finished his praises thereof with well-nigh the same sentences. But I who, by turning my eyes in another direction, showed that my mind was intent on other cares, kept my ears attentive to their discourse and received therefrom much delectable sweetness; and, as it seemed to me that I was beholden to them for such pleasure, I sometimes let my eyes rest on them more kindly and benignantly. And not once, but many times, did I perceive that some of them, puffed up with vain hopes because of this, boasted foolishly of it to their companions.

While I, then, in this way looked at a few, and that sparingly, I was myself looked at by many, and that exceedingly, and while I believed that my beauty was dazzling others, it came to pass that the beauty of another dazzled me, to my great tribulation. And now, being already close on the dolorous moment, which was fated to be the occasion either of a most assured death or of a life of such anguish that none before me has ever endured the like, prompted by I know not what spirit, I raised my eyes with decent gravity, and surveyed with penetrating look the crowds of young men who were standing near me. And I discerned, more plainly than I saw any of the others, a youth who stood directly in front of me, all alone, leaning against a marble column; and, being moved thereto by irresistible fate, I began to take thought within my mind of his bearing and manners, the which I had never before done in the case of anyone else. I say, then, that, according to my judgment, which was not at that time biased by love, he was most beautiful in form, most pleasing in deportment, and apparently of an honorable disposition. The soft and silky locks that fell in graceful curls beside his cheeks afforded manifest proof of his youthfulness. The look wherewith he eyed me seemed to beg for pity, and yet it was marked by the wariness and circumspection usual between man and man. Sure I am that I had still strength enough to turn away my eyes from his gaze, at least for a time; but no other occurrence had power to divert my attention from the things already mentioned, and upon which I had deeply pondered. And the image of his form, which was already in my mind, remained there, and this image I dwelt upon with silent delight, affirming within myself that those things were true which seemed to me to be true; and, pleased that he should look at me, I raised my eyes betimes to see whether he was still looking at me. But anon I gazed at him more steadily, making no attempt to avoid amorous snares. And when I had fixed my eyes on his more intently than was my wont, methought I could read in his eyes words which might be uttered in this wise:

"O lady, thou alone art mine only bliss!"

Certainly, if I should say that this idea was not pleasing to me, I should surely lie, for it drew forth a gentle sigh from my bosom, accompanied by these words: "And thou art mine!" unless, perchance, the words were but the echo of his, caught by my mind and remaining within it. But what availed it whether such words were spoken or not? The heart had good understanding within itself of that which was not expressed by the lips, and kept, too, within itself that which, if it had escaped outside, might, mayhap, have left me still free. And so, from that time forward, I gave more absolute liberty to my foolish eyes than ever they had possessed before, and they were well content withal. And surely, if the gods, who guide all things to a definite issue, had not deprived me of understanding, I could still have been mistress of myself. But, postponing every consideration to the last one that swayed me, I took delight in following my unruly passion, and having made myself meet, all at once, for such slavery, I became its thrall. For the fire that leaped forth from his eyes encountered the light in mine, flashing thereunto a most subtle ray. It did not remain content therewith, but, by what hidden ways I know not, penetrated directly into the deepest recesses of my heart; the which, affrighted by the sudden advent of this flame, recalled to its center its exterior forces and left me as pale as death, and also with the chill of death upon me. But not for long did this continue, rather it happened contrariwise; and I felt my heart not only glow with sudden beat, but its forces speeded back swiftly to their places, bringing with them a throbbing warmth that chased away my pallor and flushed my cheeks deeply; and, marveling wherefore this should betide, I sighed heavily; nor thereafter was there other thought in my soul than how I might please him.

In like fashion, he, without changing his place, continued to scrutinize my features, but with the greatest caution; and, perhaps, having had much practice in amorous warfare, and knowing by what devices the longed−for prey might be captured, he showed himself every moment more humble, more desperate, and more fraught with tender yearning. Alas! how much guile did that seeming desperation hide, which, as the result has now shown, though it may have come from the heart, never afterward returned to the same, and made manifest later that its revealment on the face was only a lure and a delusion! And, not to mention all his deeds, each of which was full of most artful deception, he so wrought upon me by his own craft, or else the fates willed it should so happen, that I straightway found myself enmeshed in the snares of sudden and unthought−of love, in a manner beyond all my powers of telling, and so I remain unto this very hour.

It was this one alone, therefore, most pitiful ladies, that my heart, in it mad infatuation, chose, not only among so many high−born, handsome and valiant youths then present, but even among all of the same degree having their abode in my own Parthenope, as first and last and sole lord of my life. It was this one alone that I loved, and loved more than any other. It was this one alone that was destined to be the beginning and source of my by any pleasure, although often tempted, being at last vanquished, have burned and now burn in the fire which then first caught me. Omitting many thoughts that came into my mind, and many things that were told me, I will only say that, intoxicated by a new passion, I returned with a soul enslaved to that spot whence I had gone forth in freedom.

When I was in my chamber, alone and unoccupied, inflamed with various wild wishes, filled with new sensations and throbbing with many anxieties, all of which were concentrated on the image of the youth who pleased me, I argued within myself that if I could not banish love from my luckless bosom, I might at least be able to keep cautious and secret control of it therein; and how hard it is to do such a thing, no one can discover who does not make trial of the same. Surely do I believe that not even Love himself can cause so great anguish as such an attempt is certain to produce. Furthermore, I was arrested in my purpose by the fact that I had no acquaintance with him of whom I professed myself enamored. To relate all the thoughts that were engendered in me by this love, and of what nature they were, would take altogether too much time. But some few I must perforce declare, as well as certain things that were beginning to delight me more than usual. I say, then, that, everything else being neglected, the only thing that was dear to me was the thought of my beloved, and, when it occurred to my mind that, by persevering in this course, I might, mayhap, give occasion to some one to discover that which I wished to conceal, I often upbraided myself for my folly. But what availed it all? My upbraidings had to give way to my inordinate yearning for him, and dissolved uselessly into thin air.

For several days I longed exceedingly to learn who was the youth I loved, toward whom my thoughts were ever clearly leading me; and this I craftily learned, the which filled me with great content. In like manner, the ornaments for which I had before this in no way cared, as having but little need thereof, began to be dear to me, thinking that the more I was adorned the better should I please. Wherefore I prized more than hitherto my garments, gold, pearls, and my other precious things. Until the present moment it had been my custom to frequent churches, gardens, festivals, and seaside resorts, without other wish than the companionship of young friends of my own sex; now, I sought the aforesaid places with a new desire, believing that both to see and be seen would bring me great delectation. But, in sooth, the trust which I was wont to place in my beauty had deserted me, and now I never left my chamber, without first seeking the faithful counsel of my mirror: and my hands, newly instructed thereunto by I know not what cunning master, discovering each day some more elegant mode of adornment than the day before, and deftly adding artificial charms to my natural loveliness, thereby caused me to outshine all the other ladies in my surpassing splendor. Furthermore, I began to wish for the honors usually paid to me by ladies, because of their gracious courtesy, though, perhaps, they were rather the guerdon of my noble birth, being due to me therefor, thinking that if I appeared so magnificent to my beloved's eyes, he would take the more delight in beholding me. Avarice, too, which is inborn in women, fled from me, so that I became free and openhanded, and regarded my own possessions almost as if they were not my own. The sedateness that beseems a woman fell away from me somewhat, and I grew bolder in my ways; and, in addition to all this, my eyes, which until that day looked out on the world simply and naturally, entirely changed their manner of looking, and became so artful in their office that it was a marvel. And many other alterations appeared in me over and above these, all of which I do not care to relate, for besides that the report thereof would be too tedious, I ween full well that you, like me, also have been, or are, in love, and know what changes take place in those who are in such sad case.

He was a most wary and circumspect youth, whereunto my experience was able to bear witness frequently. Going very rarely, and always in the most decorous manner, to the places where I happened to be, he used to observe me, but ever with a cautious eye, so that it seemed as if he had planned as well as I to hide the tender flames that glowed in the breasts of both. Certainly, if I denied that love, although it had clutched every corner of my heart and taken violent possession of every recess of my soul, grew even more intense whenever it happened that my eyes encountered his, I should deny the truth; he added further fuel to the fires that consumed me, and rekindled such as might be expiring, if, mayhap, there were any such. But the beginning of all this was by no means so cheerful as the ending was joyless, as soon as I was deprived of the sight of this, my beloved, inasmuch as the eyes, being thus robbed of their delight, gave woful occasion of lamentation to the heart, the sighs whereof grew greater in quality as well as in quantity, and desire, as if seizing my every feeling, took me away from myself, and, as if I were not where I was, I frequently gave him who saw me cause for amazement by affording numberless pretexts for such happenings, being taught by love itself. In addition to this, the quiet of the night and the thoughts on which my fancy fed continuously, by taking me out of myself, sometimes moved me to actions more frantic than passionate and to the employment of unusual words.

But it happened that while my excess of ornaments, heartfelt sighs, lost rest, strange actions, frantic movements, and other effects of my recent love, attracted the notice of the other domestics of the household, they especially struck with wonder a nurse of mine, old in years and experienced, and of sound judgment, who, though well aware of the flames that tortured my breast, yet making show of not knowing thereof, frequently chided me for my altered manners. One day in particular, finding me lying disconsolate on my couch, seeing that my brow was charged with doleful thoughts, and believing that we were not likely to be interrupted by other company, she began to speak as follows:

"My dearest daughter, whom I love as my very self, tell me, I pray you, what are the sorrows that have for some time past been harassing you? You who were wont to be so gay formerly, you whom I have never seen before with a mournful countenance, seem to me now to be the prey of grief and to let no moment pass without a sigh."

Then, having at first feigned to be asleep and not to have heard her, I heaved a deep sigh, and, my face, at one time flushing, at another turning pale, I tossed about on the couch, seeking what answer I should make, though, indeed, in my agitation, my tongue could hardly shape a perfect sentence. But, at length, I answered:

"Indeed, dear nurse, no fresh sorrows harass me; nor do I feel that I am in any way different from what I am wont to be. Perhaps some troubles I may have, but they are such as are incidental to all women."

"Most certainly, you are trying to deceive me, my child," returned the aged nurse, "and you seem not to reflect how serious a matter it is to attempt to lead persons of experience to believe one thing because it is couched in words and to disbelieve the opposite, although it is made plainly evident by deeds. There is no reason why you should hide from me a fact whereof I have had perfect knowledge since several days ago."

Alas! when I heard her speak thus, provoked and stung by her words, I said:

"If, then, thou wittest of all this, wherefore dost thou question me? All that thou hast to do now is to keep secret that which thou hast discovered."

"In good truth," she replied, "I will conceal all that which it is not meet that another should know, and may the earth open and engulf me in its bowels before I ever reveal aught that might turn to thy open shame! Therefore, do thou live assured of this, and guard thyself carefully from letting another know that which I, without either thyself or anyone else telling me, have learned from observing thy looks. As for myself, it is not now, but long ere now, that I have learned to keep hidden that which should not be disclosed. Therefore, do thou continue to feel secure as to this matter, and watch most carefully that thou lettest not another know that which I, not witting it from thee or from another, most surely have discovered from thine own face and from its changeful seeming. But, if thou art still the victim of that folly by which I know thou hast been enslaved, if thou art as prone now as erewhile to indulge that feeling to which thou hast already given way, then know I right well that I must leave thee to thy own devices, for bootless will be my teachings and my warnings. Still, although this cruel tyrant, to whom in thy youthful simplicity being taken by surprise thou hast yielded thy freedom, appears to have deprived thee of understanding as well as of liberty, I will put thee in mind of many things, and entreat thee to fling off and banish wicked thoughts from thy chaste bosom, to quench that unholy fire, and not to make thyself the thrall of unworthy hopes. Now is the time to be strong in resistance; for whoso makes a stout fight in the beginning roots out an unhallowed affection, and bears securely the palm of victory; but whoso, with long and wishful fancies, fosters it, will try too late to resist a yoke that has been submitted to almost unresistingly."

"Alas!" I replied, "how far easier it is to say such things than to lead them to any good result."

"Albeit they be not easy of fulfilment," she said, "yet are they possible, and they are things that it beseems you to do. Take thou thought whether it would be fitting that for such a thing as this thou shouldst lose the luster of thy exalted parentage, the great fame of thy virtue, the flower of thy beauty, the honor in which thou art now held, and, above all, the favor of the spouse whom thou hast loved and by whom thou art loved: certainly, thou shouldst not wish for this; nor do I believe thou wouldst wish it, if thou didst but weigh the matter seriously in thine own mind. Wherefore, in the name of God, forbear, and drive from thy heart the false delights promised by a guilty hope, and, with them, the madness that has seized thee. By this aged breast, long harassed by many cares, from which thou didst take thy first nutriment, I humbly beseech thee to have the courage to aid thyself, to have a concern for thine own honor, and not to disdain my warnings. Bethink thee that the very desire to be healed is itself often productive of health."

Whereto I thus made answer:

"Only too well do I know, dear nurse, the truth of that which thou sayest. But a furious madness constrains me to follow the worse course; vainly does my heart, insatiable in its desires, long for strength to enable it to adopt thy advice; what reason enjoins is rendered of no avail by this soul–subduing passion. My mind is wholly possessed by Love, who rules every part thereof, in virtue of his all–embracing deity; and surely thou art aware that his power is absolute, and 'twere useless to attempt to resist it."

Having said these words, I became almost unconscious, and fell into her arms. But she, now more agitated than before, in austere and rebuking tones, said:

"Yes, forsooth, well am I aware that you and a number of fond young women, inflamed and instigated thereunto by vain thoughts, have discovered Love to be a god, whereas a juster name for him would be that of demon; and you and they call him the son of Venus, and say that his strength has come to him from the third heaven, wishing, seemingly, to offer necessity as an excuse for your foolishness. Oh, was ever woman so misled as thou? Truly, thou must be bereft entirely of understanding! What a thing thou sayest! Love a deity! Love is a madness, thrust forth from hell by some fury. He speeds across the earth in hasty flight, and they whom he visits soon discover that he brings no deity with him, but frenzy rather; yet none will he visit except those abounding overmuch in earthly felicity; for they, he knows, in their overweening conceit, are ready to afford him lodgment and shelter. This has been proven to us by many facts. Do we not see that Venus, the true, the heavenly Venus, often dwells in the humblest cot, her sole concern being the perpetuation of our race? But this god, whom some in their folly name Love, always hankering after things unholy, ministers only to those whose fortunes are prosperous. This one, recoiling from those whose food and raiment suffice to meet the demands of nature, uses his best efforts to win over the pampered and the splendidly attired, and with their food and their habiliments he mixes his poisons, and so gains the lordship of their wicked souls; and, for this reason, he gladly seeks a harborage in lofty palaces, and seldom, or rather never, enters the houses of the lowly, because this horrible plague always resorts by choice to scenes of elegance and refinement, well knowing that such places are best fitted for the achievement of his fell purposes. It is easy for us to see that among the humble the affections are sane and well ordered; but the rich, on the other hand, everywhere pluming themselves on their riches, and being insatiable in their pursuit of other things as well as of wealth, always show more eagerness therein than is becoming; and they who can do much desire furthermore to have the power of doing that which they must not do: among whom I feel that thou hast placed thyself, O most hapless of women, seeing that thou hast already entered and traveled far on a path that will surely lead to guilt and misery."

After hearing which, I said:

"Be silent, old woman, and provoke not the wrath of the gods by thy speech. Now that thou art incapacitated from love by age and rejected by all the gods, thou railest against this one, blaspheming him in whom thou didst erstwhile take delight. If other ladies, far more puissant, famous, and wise than I, have formerly called him by that name, it is not in my power to give him a name anew. By him am I now truly enslaved; whatever be the cause of this, and whether it be the occasion of my happiness or misery, I am helpless. The strength wherewith I once opposed him has been vanquished and has abandoned me. Therefore either death or the youth for whom I languish can alone end my tortures. If thou art, then, as wise as I hold thee to be, bestow such counsel and help on me as may lighten my anguish, or, at least, abstain from exasperating it by censuring that to which my soul, unable to act differently, is inclined with all its energy."

Thereupon, she, being angry, and not without reason, making no answer, but muttering to herself, passed out of the chamber and left me alone.

When my dear nurse had departed without making further discourse, and I was again alone, I felt that I had acted ill in despising her advice. I revolved her sayings within my restless breast; and, albeit my understanding was blinded, I perceived that what she had said was replete with wisdom, and, almost repenting of what I had uttered and of the course which I had declared I purposed taking, I was wavering in my mind. And, already beginning to have thoughts of abandoning that course which was sure to be in every way most harmful, I was about to call her back to give me encouragement, when a new and unforeseen event suddenly changed my intention. For a most beautiful lady, come to my private chamber I know not whence, presented herself before my eyes, enveloped in such dazzling light that scarcely could my sight endure the brightness thereof. But while she stood still and silent before me, the effulgent radiance that had almost blinded my vision, after a time left it unobscured, and I was able so to portray her every aspect to my mind, as her whole beauteous figure was impressed on my memory. I saw that she was nude, except for a thin and delicate drapery of purple, which, albeit in some parts it covered the milk–white body, yet no more concealed it from my ravished eyes than does the transparent glass conceal the portrait beneath it. Her head, the hair whereof as much surpassed gold in its luster as gold surpasses the yellowest tresses to be found among mortals, was garlanded with a wreath of green myrtle, beneath whose shadow I beheld two eyes of peerless splendor, so enchanting that I could have gazed on them forever; they flashed forth such luminous beams that it was a marvel; and all the rest of her countenance had such transcendent loveliness that the like never was seen here below. At first she spake no word, perchance content that I should look upon her, or perchance seeing me so content to look upon her. Then gradually through the translucent radiance, she revealed more clearly every hidden grace, for she was aware that I could not believe such beauty possible except I beheld it with my eyes, and that even then words would fail me to picture it to mortals with my tongue. At last, when she observed that I had sated my eyes with gazing on her, and when she saw that her coming hither was as wondrous to me as her loveliness, with smiling face, and in a voice sweeter than can be conceived by minds like ours, she thus addressed me:

"Prithee, young woman, what art thou, the most fickle of thy sex, preparing to do in obedience to the late counsels of thy aged nurse? Knowest thou not that such counsels are far harder to follow than that very love which thou desirest to flee? Hast thou reflected on the dire and unendurable torments which compliance with them will entail on thee? O most insensate one! dost thou then, who only a few hours ago wert my willing vassal, now wish to break away from my gentle rule, because, forsooth, of the words of an old woman, who is no longer vassal of mine, as if, like her, thou art now unwitting of what delights I am the source? O most witless of women! forbear, and reflect whether thou shouldst not find befitting happiness in that which makes the happiness of Heaven and earth. All things that Phoebus beholds during the bright day, from what time he emerges from Ganges, until he plunges with his tired steeds into the Hesperian waves, to seek due repose after his wearisome pilgrimage; all things that are confined between cold Arcturus and the red–hot pole, all own the absolute and authentic lordship of my winged son; and in Heaven not only is he esteemed a god, like the other deities, but he is so much more puissant than them all that not one remains who has not heretofore been vanquished by his darts. He, flying on golden plumage throughout his realms, with such swiftness that his passage can hardly be discerned, visits them all in turn, and, bending his strong bow, to the drawn string he fits the arrows forged by me and tempered in the fountains sacred to my divinity. And when he elects anyone to his service, as being more worthy than others, that one he rules as it likes him. He kindles raging fires in the hearts of the young, fans the flames that are almost dead in the old, awakens the fever of passion in the chaste bosoms of virgins and instils a genial warmth into the breasts of wives and widows

21

equally. He has even aforetime forced the gods, wrought up to a frenzy by his blazing torch, to forsake the heavens and dwell on earth under false appearances. Whereof the proofs are many. Was not Phoebus, though victor over huge Python and creator of the celestial strains that sound from the lyres of Parnassus, by him made the thrall, now of Daphne, now of Clymene, and again of Leucothea, and of many others withal? Certainly, this was so. And, finally, hiding his brightness under the form of a shepherd, did not Apollo tend the flocks of Admetus? Even Jove himself, who rules the skies, by this god coerced, molded his greatness into forms inferior to his own. Sometimes, in shape of a snow–white fowl, he gave voice to sounds sweeter than those of the dying swan, and anon, changing to a young bull and fitting horns to his brow, he bellowed along the plains, and humbled his proud flanks to the touch of a virgin's knees, and, compelling his tired hoofs to do the office of oars, he breasted the waves of his brother's kingdom, yet sank not in its depths, but joyously bore away his prize. I shall not discourse unto you of his pursuit of Semele under his proper form, or of Alcmena, in guise of Amphitryon, or of Callisto, under the semblance of Diana, or of Danae for whose sake he became a shower of gold, seeing that in the telling thereof I should waste too much time. Nay, even the savage god of war, whose strength appalls the giants, repressed his wrathful bluster, being forced to such submission by this my son, and became gentle and loving. And the forger of Jupiter, and artificer of his three–pronged thunderbolts, though trained to handle fire, was smitten by a shaft more potent than he himself had ever wrought. Nay I, though I be his mother, have not been able to fend off his arrows: Witness the tears I have shed for the death of Adonis! But why weary myself and thee with the utterance of so many words? There is no deity in heaven who has passed unscathed from his assaults; except, perhaps, Diana only, who may have escaped him by fleeing to the woods; though some there be who tell that she did not flee, but rather concealed the wound. If haply, however, thou, in the hardness of thy unbelief, rejectest the testimony of heaven, and searchest rather for examples of those in this nether world who have felt his power, I affirm them to be so multitudinous that where to begin I know not. Yet this much may I tell thee truly: all who have confessed his sway have been men of might and valor. Consider attentively, in the first place, that undaunted son of Alcmena, who, laying aside his arrows and the formidable skin of the huge lion, was fain to adorn his fingers with green emeralds, and to smooth and adjust his bristling and rebellions hair. Nay, that hand which aforetime had wielded the terrific club, and slain therewith Antaeus, and dragged the hound of hell from the lower world, was now content to draw the woolen threads spun from Omphale's distaff; and the shoulders whereon had rested the pillars of the heavens, from which he had for a time freed Atlas, were now clasped in Omphale's arms, and afterward, to do her pleasure, covered with a diaphanous raiment of purple. Need I relate what Paris did in obedience to the great deity? or Helen? or Clytemnestra? or AEgisthus? These are things that are well known to all the world. Nor do I care to speak of Achilles, or of Scylla, of Ariadne or Leander, of Dido, or of many others, of whom the same tale could be told, were there need to tell it. Believe me when I affirm that this fire is holy, and most potent as well. Thou hast heard that heaven and earth are subject to my son because of his lordship over gods and men. But what shall I say of the power that he exercises over irrational animals, whether celestial or terrene? It is through him that the turtle is fain to follow her mate; it is through him that my pigeons have learned to caress his ringdoves with fondest endearments. And there is no creeping or living creature that has ever at any time attempted to escape from his puissance: in the woods the timid stag, made fierce by his touch, becomes brave for sake of the coveted hind and by bellowing and fighting, they prove how strong are the witcheries of Love. The ferocious boars are made by Love to froth at the mouth and sharpen their ivory tusks; the African lions, when Love quickens them, shake their manes in fury. But leaving the groves and forests, I assert that even in the chilly waters the numberless divinities of the sea and of the flowing rivers are not safe from the bolts of my son. Neither can I for a moment believe that thou art ignorant of the testimony thereof which has been rendered by Neptune, Glaucus, Alpheus, and others too numerous to mention: not only were they unable to quench the flame with their dank waters, but they could not even moderate its fury, which, when it had made its might felt, both on the earth and in the waters, continued its onward course, and rested not until it had penetrated into the gloomy realms of Dis. Therefore Heaven and Earth and Ocean and Hell itself have had experience of the potency of his weapons. And, in order that thou mayest understand in a few words the power of the deity, I tell thee that, while everything succumbs to nature, and nothing can ever be emancipated from her dominion, Nature herself is but the servant of Love. When he commands, ancient hatreds perish, and angry moods, be they old or new, give place to his fires; and lastly, his sway has such far-reaching influence that even stepmothers become gracious to their stepchildren, a thing which it is a marvel to behold. Therefore what seekest thou? Why dost thou hesitate? Why dost thou rashly avoid him? When so many gods, when so many men, when so many animals, have been vanquished by him, art ashamed to be vanquished by him also? In good sooth, thou weenest not what thou art doing. If thou fearest to be blamed for thy obedience to him, a blame so unmerited never can be thy portion. Greater sins than thou canst commit have been committed by thousands far greater than thou, and these sins would plead as thy excuse, shouldst thou pursue that course which others have pursued—others who far excel thee. Thou wilt have sinned but a little, seeing that thou hadst far less power of resistance than those aforementioned. But if my words move thee not, and thou wouldst still wish to withstand the god, bethink thee that thy power falls far short of that of Jove, and that in judgment thou canst not equal Phoebus, nor in wealth Juno, nor me in beauty; and yet, we all have been conquered. Thou art greatly deceived, and I fear me that thou must perish in the end, if thou persist in thy changed purpose. Let that which has erstwhile sufficed for the whole world, suffice for thee, nor try to render thyself cold-hearted, by saying: 'I have a husband, and the holy laws and the vowed faith forbid me this'; for bootless are such reasonings against the puissance of this god. He discards the laws of others scornfully, as thinking them of no account, and ordains his own. Pasiphae? had a husband, and Phaedra, and I, too, even though I have loved. And it is these same husbands who most frequently fall in love with others, albeit they have wives of their own: witness Jason and Theseus and valiant Hector and Ulysses. Therefore to men we do no wrong if we apply to them the same laws that they apply to others; for to them no privilege has been granted which is not accorded to us withal. Banish, then, thy foolish thoughts, and, in all security, go on loving him whom thou hadst already begun to love. In good sooth, if thou refusest to own the power of mighty Love, it behooves thee to fly; but whither canst thou fly? Knowest thou of any retreat where he will not follow and overtake thee? He has in all places equal puissance. Go wheresoever thou wilt, never canst thou pass across the borders of his realms, and within these realms vain it is for mortals to try to hide themselves when he would smite them. But let it comfort thee to know, young woman, that no such odious passion shall trouble thee as erstwhile was the scourge of Myrrha, Semiramis, Byblis, Canace, and Cleopatra. Nothing strange or new will be wrought by my son in thy regard. He has, as have the other gods, his own special laws, which thou art not the first to obey, and shouldst not be the last to entertain hopes therefrom. If haply thou believest that thou art without companions in this, foolish is thy belief. Let us pass by the other world, which is fraught with such happenings; but observe attentively only thine own city! What an infinite number of ladies it can show who are in the same case with thyself! And remember that what is done by so many cannot be deemed unseemly. Therefore, be thou of our following, and return thanks to our beauty, which thou hast so closely examined. But return special thanks to our deity, which has sundered thee from the ranks of the simple, and persuaded thee to become acquainted with the delights that our gifts bestow."

Alas! alas! ye tender and compassionate ladies, if Love has been propitious to your desires, say what could I, what should I, answer to such and so great words uttered by so great a goddess, if not: "Be it done unto me according to thy pleasure"? And so, I affirm that as soon as she had closed her lips, having already harvested within my understanding all her words, and feeling that every word was charged with ample excuse for what I might do, and knowing now how mighty she was and how resistless, I resolved at once to submit to her guidance; and instantly rising from my couch, and kneeling on the ground, with humbled heart, I thus began, in abashed and tremulous accents:

"O peerless and eternal loveliness! O divinest of deities! O sole mistress of all my thoughts! whose power is felt to be most invincible by those who dare to try to withstand it, forgive the ill–timed obstinacy wherewith I, in my great folly, attempted to ward off from my breast the weapons of thy son, who was then to me an unknown divinity. Now, I repeat, be it done unto me according to thy pleasure, and according to thy promises withal. Surely, my faith merits a due reward in time and space, seeing that I, taking delight in thee more than do all other women, wish to see the number of thy subjects increase forever and ever."

Hardly had I made an end of speaking these words, when she moved from the place where she was standing, and came toward me. Then, her face glowing with the most fervent expression of affection and sympathy, she embraced me, and touched my forehead with her divine lips. Next, just as the false Ascanius, when panting in the arms of Dido, breathed on her mouth, and thereby kindled the latent flame, so did she breathe on my mouth, and, in that wise, rendered the divine fire that slumbered in my heart more uncontrollable than ever, and this I felt at that very moment. Thereafter, opening a little her purple robe, she showed me, clasped in her arms against her ravishing breast, the very counterpart of the youth I loved, wrapped in the transparent folds of a Grecian mantle, and revealing in the lineaments of his countenance pangs that were not unlike those I suffered.

"O damsel," she said, "rivet thy gaze on the youth before thee: we have not given thee for lover a Lissa, a Geta, or a Birria, or anyone resembling them, but a person in every way worthy of being loved by every goddess in the heavens. Thee he loves more than himself, as we have ordained, and thee will he ever love; therefore do thou, joyfully and securely, abandon thyself to his love. Thy prayers have moved us to pity, as it is meet that prayers so deserving should, and so, be of good hope, and fear not that thou shalt be without the reward due thee in the future."

La Fiammetta

And thereafter she suddenly vanished from my eyes. *Oime!* wretched me! I do not for a moment doubt now, after considering the things which followed, that this one who appeared unto me was not Venus, but rather Tisiphone, who, doffing from her head the horrid snakes that served it for hair, and assuming for the while the splendid form of the Goddess of Love, in this manner lured me with deceitful counsels to that disaster which at length overwhelmed me. Thus did Juno, but in different fashion, veiling the radiance of her deity and transforming herself for the occasion into the exact likeness of her aged nurse, persuaded Semele to her undoing. Woe is me! my resolve to be so advised was the cause—O hallowed Modesty! O Chastity, most sacred of all the virtues! sole and most precious treasure of righteous women!—was the cause, I repeat, wherefore I drove ye from my bosom. Yet do I venture to pray unto ye for pardon, and surely the sinner who repents and perseveres in repentance should in due season obtain your forgiveness.

Although the goddess had disappeared from my sight, my whole soul, nevertheless, continued to crave her promised delights; and, albeit the ardor of the passion that vexed my soul deprived me of every other feeling, one piece of good fortune, for what deserving of mine I know not, remained to me out of so many that had been lost—namely, the power of knowing that seldom if ever has a smooth and happy ending been granted to love, if that love be divulged and blazed abroad. And for this reason, when influenced by my highest thoughts, I resolved, although it was a most serious thing to do so, not to set will above reason in carrying this my desire unto an ending. And assuredly, although I have often been most violently constrained by divers accidents to follow certain courses, yet so much grace was conceded to me that, sustained by my own firmness, I passed through these agonies without revealing the pangs that tortured me. And in sooth, I have still resolution enough to continue to follow out this my purpose; so that, although the things I write are most true, I have so disposed them that no one, however keen his sagacity, can ever discover who I am, except him who is as well acquainted with these matters as I, being, indeed, the occasion of them all. And I implore him, should this little book ever come into his hands, in the name of that love which he once bore me, to conceal that which, if disclosed, would turn neither to his profit nor honor. And, albeit he has deprived me of himself, and that through no fault of mine, let him not take it upon himself to deprive me of that honor which I still possess, although, perchance, undeservedly; for should he do so, he could never again give it back to me, any more than he can now give me back himself.

La Fiammetta

Having, therefore, formed my plans in this wise, I showed the most long-suffering patience in manifesting my keenest and most covetous yearnings, and I used my best efforts, but only in secret ways and when opportunities were afforded me, to light in this young man's soul the same flames wherewith my own soul glowed, and to make him as circumspect as myself withal. Nor, in truth, was this for me a task of great difficulty; for, inasmuch as the lineaments of the face always bear most true witness to the qualities of the heart, it was not long before I became aware that my desire would have its full fruition. I perceived that, not only was he throbbing with amorous enthusiasm, but that he was also imbued with most perfect discretion, and this was exceedingly pleasing to me. He, being at once wishful to preserve my honor in all its luster, and, at the same time, to arrange convenient times and places for our meetings, employed many ingenious stratagems, which, methinks, must have cost him much toil and trouble. He used every subtle art to win the friendship of all who were related to me, and, at last, of my husband; and not only did he enjoy their friendship, but he possessed it in such a supreme degree that no pleasure was agreeable to them unless he shared it. How much all this delighted me you will understand without its being needful to me to set it down in words. And is there anyone so dull of wit as not to conclude that from the aforesaid friendship arose many opportunities for him and me of holding discourse together in public? But already had he bethought himself of acting in more subtle ways; and now he would speak to this one, now to that one, words whereby I, being most eager for such enlightenment, discovered that whatever he said to these was fraught with figurative and hidden meanings, intended to show forth his ardent affection for myself. When he was sensible that I had a clear perception of the occult significance of his questions and answers, he went still further, and by gestures, and mobile changes in the expression of his features, he would make known to me his thoughts and the various phases of his passion, which was to me a source of much delectation; and I strove so hard to comprehend it all and to make fitting response thereunto, that neither could he shadow forth anything to me, nor I to him, that either of us did not at once understand.

Nay, not satisfied even with this, he employed other symbols and metaphors, and labored earnestly to discipline me in such manner of speech; and, to render me the more assured of his unalterable love, he named me Fiammetta, and himself Panfilo. Woe is me! How often, when warmed with love and wine, did we tell tales, in the presence of our dearest friends, of Fiammetta and Panfilo, feigning that they were Greeks of the days of old, I at one time, he at another; and the tales were all of ourselves; how we were first caught in the snares of Love, and of what tribulations we were long the victims, giving suitable

27

names to the places and persons connected with the story! Certainly, I frequently laughed at it all, being made merry by the simplicity of the bystanders, as well as by his astuteness and sagacity. Yet betimes I dreaded that in the flush of his excitement he might thoughtlessly let his tongue wander in directions wherein it was not befitting it should venture. But he, being ever far wiser than I imagined, guarded himself craftily from any such blundering awkwardness.

Oime! most compassionate ladies, what is there that Love will not teach to his subjects? and what is there that he is not able to render them skilful in learning? I, who of all young women was the most simple−minded, and ordinarily with barely power to loose my tongue, when among my companions, concerning the most trivial and ordinary affairs, now, because of this my affection, mastered so speedily all his modes of speech that, in a brief space, my aptness at feigning and inventing surpassed that of any poet! And there were few questions put to me in response to which, after meditating on their main points, I could not make up a pleasing tale: a thing, in my opinion, exceedingly difficult for a young woman to begin, and still more difficult to finish and relate afterward. But, if my actual situation required it, I might set down numerous details which might, perhaps, seem to you of little or no moment, as, for instance, the artful experiment whereby we tested the fidelity of my favorite maid to whom, and to whom alone, we meditated entrusting the secret of this hidden passion, considering that, should another share it, our uneasiness, lest it should not be kept, would be most grievous. Furthermore, it would weary you if I mentioned all the plans we adopted, in order to meet divers situations, plans that I do not believe were ever imagined by any before us; and albeit I am now well aware that they all worked for my ultimate destruction, yet the remembrance of them does not displease me.

Unless, O ladies, my judgment be greatly at fault, the strength of our minds was by no means small, if it be but taken in account how hard a thing it is for youthful persons in love to resist long the rush of impetuous ardor without crossing the bounds set by reason: nay, it was so great and of such quality that the most valiant of men, by acting in such wise, would win high and worthy laud as a result thereof. But my pen is now about to depict the final ending to which love was guided, and, before I do so, I would appeal to your pity and to those soft sentiments which make their dwelling in your tender breasts, and incline your thoughts to a like termination.

La Fiammetta

Day succeeded day, and our wishes dragged along with them, kept alive by torturing anxiety, the full bitterness whereof each of us experienced; although the one manifested this to the other in disguised language, and the other showed herself over–discreet to an excessive degree; all of which you who know how ladies who are beloved behave in such circumstances will easily understand. Well, then, he, putting full trust in the veiled meaning of my words, and choosing the proper time and place, came to an experience of that which I desired as much as he, although I feigned the contrary. Certainly, if I were to say that this was the cause of the love I felt for him, I should also have to confess that every time it came back to my memory, it was the occasion to me of a sorrow like unto none other. But, I call God to witness, nothing that has happened between us had the slightest influence upon the love I bore him, nor has it now. Still, I will not deny that our close intimacy was then, and is now, most dear to me. And where is the woman so unwise as not to wish to have the object of her affection within reach rather than at a distance? How much more intensely does love enthrall us when it is brought so near us that we and it are made almost inseparable! I say, then, that after such an adventure, never afore willed or even thought of by me, not once, but many times did fortune and our adroit stratagems bring us good cheer and consolation, not indeed screened entirely from danger, for which I cared less than for the passing of the fleeing wind. But while the time was being spent in such joyous fashion—and that it was joyous, Love, who alone may bear witness thereof, can truly say—yet sometimes his coming inspired me with not a little natural apprehension, inasmuch as he was beginning to be indiscreet in the manner of his coming. But how dear to him was my own apartment, and with what gladness did it see him enter! Yet was he filled with more reverence for it than he ever had been for a sacred temple, and this I could at all times easily discern. Woe is me! what burning kisses, what tender embraces, what delicious moments we had there!

Why do I take such pleasure in the mere words which I am now setting down? It is, I say, because I am forced to express the gratitude I then felt to the holy goddess who was the promiser and bestower of Love's delights. Ah, how often did I visit her altars and offer incense, crowned with a garland of her favorite foliage! How often did I think scornfully of the counsels of my aged nurse! Nay, furthermore, being elated far more than all my other companions, how often did I disparage their loves, saying within myself: "No one is loved as I am loved, no one loves a youth as matchless as the youth I love, no one realizes such delights from love as I!" In short, I counted the world as nothing in comparison with my love. It seemed to me that my head touched the skies, and that nothing was lacking to the culmination of my ecstatic bliss. Betimes the idea flashed on my mind that I must disclose to others the occasion of my transports, for surely, I would reflect, it would be a delight to others to hear of that which has brought such delight to me! But thou, O Shame, on the one side, and thou, O Fear, on the other, did hold me back: the one threatening me with eternal infamy; the other with loss of that which hostile Fortune was soon afterward to tear from me. In such wise then, did I live for some time, for it was then pleasing to Love that I should live in this manner; and, in good sooth, so blithely and joyously were these days spent that I had little cause to envy any lady in the whole world, never imagining that the delight wherewith my heart was filled to overflowing, was to nourish the root and plant of my future misery, as I now know to my fruitless and never-ending sorrow.